The Halloween Class

by Peter Maloney
and Felicia Zekauskas

SCHOLASTIC INC.

New York   Toronto   London   Auckland   Sydney
Mexico City   New Delhi   Hong Kong   Buenos Aires

To Amy Peterson

ISBN 0-439–39519-4

Library of Congress Cataloging-in-Publication Data available

12 11 10 9 8 7 6 5 4 3 2   2 3 4 5 6 7/0

Printed in the U.S.A. • First printing, October 2002 • Book design by Mark Freiman

CHAPTER 1
A Scary Class

Mrs. Robinson walked into her classroom. She couldn't believe her eyes!

All of her students — Peter and
Felicia, Tobi and Rich, Russ Deluca,
and everyone else — were gone!

Instead, there were wizards and
witches, ghosts and goblins,
pirates and princesses.
And there was one empty seat.

"I must be in the wrong room," said Mrs. Robinson.

Then she saw the calendar on the wall.
It was October 31.

"You scared me!" said Mrs. Robinson.
"I forgot today was Halloween."

Chapter 2
Who's Who?

"Let's see if I can guess who's who," said Mrs. Robinson. "I'll close my eyes. Everyone change seats."

Mrs. Robinson closed her eyes
and slowly counted to ten.
All the children switched places.

"Okay!" said Mrs. Robinson.
"Let's see who's who." She looked at
the monster in the first row.

"Russ Deluca!"
she said.

"The cupid
with the bow
and arrows—
that's Felicia.

And the fireman in the
third row, that's Rich."

Mrs. Robinson went
up and down each row.

"Wow, you're good!" said Tobi.

CHAPTER 3
How Did You Do That?

Mrs. Robinson had guessed that Tobi was the ladybug in the back row. "How did you know it was me?" Tobi asked.

"The costumes we choose tell a lot about us," Mrs. Robinson said. "I know how much you like bugs, Tobi. It was easy to guess that you might dress up as one."

"How did you guess me?"
asked Felicia.
"Your bow gave you away,"
said Mrs. Robinson.

"My bow?!" said Felicia.
"I thought cupids always
carried a bow."

"I meant your *hair* bow."
Mrs. Robinson laughed.
"You always wear one."

16

Chapter 4
Someone's Missing

Mrs. Robinson was perfect. She guessed everyone — except for one.
"Where's Peter?" she asked. "I don't see him anywhere."

"I saw him walking to school today," said Russ Deluca. "He was dressed in white bandages from head to toe. I think he was a mummy."

"He wasn't a mummy," said Felicia.
"He was the . . . the . . . the . . ."
"The *what*?" asked Mrs. Robinson.
"I can't say," said Felicia. "I promised
Peter that I wouldn't tell anyone."

"Look!" cried Tobi. Everyone turned around. A pile of white bandages lay by an empty desk. Then everyone turned to look at Felicia.

"Felicia, I think you should tell us what you know," said Mrs. Robinson. "Sometimes it's more important to break a promise than to keep it."

CHAPTER 5
The Invisible Boy

"Oh, all right," said Felicia.
"Peter was the . . . the . . . the . . ."

"THE INVISIBLE BOY!" shouted a voice that came out of nowhere.

Everyone stared at the pile of bandages.

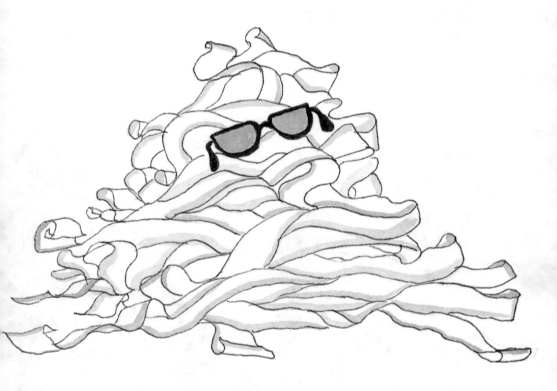

"What was that?" cried Tobi.
"I am THE INVISIBLE BOY!"
repeated the voice.

Mrs. Robinson looked shocked.
Russ Deluca's mouth dropped open.
And everyone looked a little scared.

"Peter, where are you?" asked Mrs.
Robinson. "Why can't we see you?"

"You can't see me," said the voice, "because I am **THE INVISIBLE BOY!**"

"That's enough!" said Mrs. Robinson. "The Invisible Boy is make-believe. Please show yourself right now."

"Okay," said the voice. Suddenly,
the doors to the coat closet opened.
There was Peter.

"That was some trick, young man," said Mrs. Robinson. "You scared me more than all the wizards, witches, ghosts, and goblins in this room!"

CHAPTER 6
How Did *You* Do That?

After school, Peter and Felicia walked home together.
"How did you make yourself disappear?" Felicia asked.

"It was easy," said Peter. "If you give me some of your gummy bears, I'll show you."

"Sure," said Felicia. She opened her backpack and started digging for gummy bears. When she looked up, Peter was gone!

"Peter, where are you?" she shouted.
"I'm right here," boomed the voice.
"I am **THE INVISIBLE BOY!**"
Felicia couldn't believe her eyes.
Peter had disappeared again!

Then Felicia saw a red sneaker.
It was poking out from behind a bush.
"Are you sure you're invisible?"
asked Felicia.
"That's what I said," boomed the voice.

"Then this shouldn't bother you,"
she said.

Felicia jumped in the air and landed
on the red sneaker.
"Ouch!" cried Peter. He leaped out
from behind the bush, hopping up and
down on one foot.
"I guess I had that coming," said Peter.

"Either *you* had it coming," said
Felicia, "or the Invisible Boy did!"